Disney's
Winnie the Pooh
Friendship Day

Friendship equals caring,

In very special ways—

For friends

Are always there,

Not just on

"Friendship Days"!

E verybody in the Hundred-Acre Wood was getting ready for Friendship Day. There was going to be a great celebration with lots of games, food, and fun for all.

Piglet visited Pooh and helped him fill some honey pots.
Pooh felt so happy, he hummed a little tune:
"Honey in my tummy is yummy-yum-yummy!"

"What are you doing with these honey pots?" asked Piglet.
"I'm giving them out on Friendship Day," Pooh replied,
"because good friends are as sweet as honey."

Soon Pooh and Piglet took a walk through the Wood and found
Christopher Robin hard at work.

"What are you making, Christopher Robin?" asked Pooh.

"Hats to wear on Friendship Day," he replied.

Pooh tried on a hat for Christopher Robin, who made one last little snip and tuck.

"I can't wait to wear my hat on Friendship Day," Pooh replied.

Soon the friends said goodbye, and Pooh and Piglet went to Owl's house.

Owl was busy picking out a story about friendship.

"Which one do you think I should read?" Owl asked, pointing to a tall stack of books.

"Perhaps you should read them all," said Pooh.

"That's a splendid idea!" Owl cried. "Simply splendid."

Next, Pooh and Piglet passed by Roo's house.
"Friends can be new; friends can be old!
But all of them are as precious as gold," sang Roo.
Pooh and Piglet called "hello" through the window.

Roo came running outside. "Mama was just teaching me a song for Friendship Day," he explained.

"I know what we're all doing for Friendship Day," said Piglet. "But I wonder about Rabbit."

"Let's go see," Pooh suggested.

When the three friends got to Rabbit's house, they oohed and ahhed at the wonderful smells swirling through his kitchen.

"It's my secret recipe for Friendship Stew," Rabbit said.

"What's in it?" asked Roo.

"Well, er. . .if I tell you, then it won't be my *secret* recipe anymore," Rabbit explained.

"What are you doing for Friendship Day, Piglet?" asked Rabbit, changing the subject.

"I'm baking my friendliest haycorn cookies," Piglet replied.

Pooh, Piglet, and Roo said goodbye to Rabbit and continued on their way. Soon they ran into Tigger.

"Hoo-hoo-hoo," called Tigger. "I'm practicing for the Friendship Day bouncing contest!"

Tigger stopped just long enough to give Piglet, Pooh, and Roo each a really good bounce. BOING, BOING, BOING!

"Yupperee!" Tigger cried. "Bouncing is what tiggers do best! See ya later, Buddy Boys!"

Next the three friends visited Eeyore in his thistle patch.
"What are you doing for Friendship Day?" Roo asked Eeyore.
"Still trying to think of something," Eeyore replied.

"You could lend us your tail for our relay race," said Roo.
"Or use your tail to pull our friendship wagon," Piglet piped up.
"I would," Eeyore replied, "but I seem to have lost it again."

"We hope you think of something soon!" Roo said.
"But if you don't, please come anyway," added Piglet.
"It wouldn't be Friendship Day without you," said Pooh.

When Friendship Day arrived, Christopher Robin hurried over to Pooh's house carrying his hats. He bumped right into Eeyore. "Why don't you come with me?" Christopher Robin asked.

"I'm not going to Friendship Day," Eeyore replied.
"Why not?" asked Christopher Robin.
"Couldn't find anything 'friendly' to do," he shrugged.

"A friend doesn't have to do anything except let others know he cares," Christopher Robin explained. "Why, I'd say you're a 'prizewinning' friend."

"I always thought my friends were sorta prizewinning," said Eeyore.

Suddenly Eeyore had a wonderful idea! First he asked Christopher Robin for a long roll of ribbon. Then the two friends made everyone in the Hundred-Acre Wood their very own award.

Later that day, Eeyore showed up carrying a large sack on his back. When it was time, Christopher Robin announced that Eeyore had something special to share with all his friends.

Eeyore shyly handed out the ribbons one at a time.

"I say, Eeyore," Owl announced. "This is one of the best Friendship Day gifts a friend could receive."

"Let the celebration begin!" Christopher Robin cried.

And so the group had a wonderful time sharing their gifts and singing their songs. But the best part of Friendship Day was that all of the friends could be together.

A LESSON A DAY
POOH'S WAY

Caring is what

Friendship is all about.